MORE
LIFE'S LIT
DESTRUCTIO

A Parody

By Charles Sherwood Dane

A Stonesong Press Book
St. Martin's Press   New York

MORE LIFE'S LITTLE DESTRUCTION BOOK

Copyright © 1993 by The Stonesong Press, Inc.

All rights reserved. No part of this book may be used or reproduced in any manner whatsoever without written permission except in the case of brief quotations embodied in critical articles or reviews. For information, write to St. Martin's Press, 175 Fifth Avenue, New York, N.Y. 10010.

ISBN: 0-312-95206-6

Typeset by *RECAP:* Publications, Inc.

Printed in the United States of America

St. Martin's Paperbacks edition / July 1993

10 9 8 7 6 5 4 3 2 1

INTRODUCTION

All right, all right. We heard you! All the clamor for this new collection of mean and rotten ways to make everyone miserable. It just goes to prove what we've been saying all along: You can't have too much of a bad thing.

Maybe we've softened but we've added two additional bonuses for you:

1) Little White Lies you can tell to cover your you know what, and

2) A bunch of ways to make yourself totally miserable. We call these Self Destructions.

Now go out there and make us proud!

We reluctantly must thank again all who contributed to this little lampoon. They are, in no particular order, Ned Bienemann, Sheree Bykofsky, David Dinin, Christopher Fargis, Paul Fargis, Victoria Gallucci, Caroline McKeldin, Adam O'Conner, Lea Bayers Rapp, Tricia Reinus, Celine Texier Rose, Wendy Silbert, and Jennifer Weis.

513 ❖ Carry a grudge.

514 ❖ Wait until you're in the voting booth to decide.

515 ❖ Cross your leg over and keep shaking your foot.

516 ❖ Emulate Bart Simpson.

517 ❖ Whatever it is, be against it.

518 ❖ Power Trip.

519 ❖ Be first on the bus,
then grope around
for change.

520 ❖ Bring an uninvited guest to the wedding.

521 ❖ Keep the car behind you from making the light.

522 ❖ Pretend you didn't hear the question.

523 ❖ Before you give that hearty handshake, sneeze into your hand.

524 ❖ Tell kids, "Sleep tight; don't let the bed bugs bite."

525 ❖ When you do something bad, use someone else's name.

526 ❖ When you're in a foreign country, refuse to speak the language.

527 ❖ When the collection basket is passed to you, help yourself.

528 ❖ At a convention, stare at people's badges when you talk to them.

529 ❖ Assign blame.

530 ❖ Raise your voice so that people who don't speak English will understand you.

531 ❖ Develop a truly blank look.

532 ❖ Drool.

533 ❖ Get drunk before PTA meetings.

534 ❖ Staple check to billing statement before mailing.

535 ❖ Walk on freshly seeded areas.

536 ❖ Eavesdrop.

537 ❖ Blow your horn as soon as the light turns green.

538 ❖ Blow your stack.

539 ❖ Paint your fingernails on the airplane.

540 ❖ Seduce a superior, and then claim sexual harassment.

541 ❖ House an illegal alien.

542 ❖ Turn up the volume on late movies.

543 ❖ Rub everyone the wrong way.

544 ❖ Actually chill out.

545 ❖ Begin a job interview by asking about the holidays.

546 ❖ Poke kids playfully in their bellybuttons.

547 ❖ Tell your hostess her dishes are dirty.

548 ❖ Brush your hair in the kitchen.

549 ❖ Dampen spirits and edit out joy.

550 ❖ Serve runny eggs.

551 ❖ Use a bullhorn to call the umpire obscene names.

552 ❖ Strive to be politically perfect, not just politically correct.

553 ❖ Go to the concert with a hacking cough.

554 ❖ When the pianist pauses, applaud.

555 ❖ Scratch your crotch in public.

556 ❖ Breastfeed your twins at the stadium.

557 ❖ Be one of the guys who just doesn't get it.

558 ❖ Show people where they went wrong.

559 ❖ Stare at the chests of big-breasted women.

560 ❖ Insist you were there first.

561 ❖ Remember, all's fair in love and war.

562 ❖ Proselytize your cult.

563 ❖ Send gifts C.O.D.

564 ❖ Be redundant, time and time again.

565 ❖ Talk in rhyme all the time.

566 ❖ Never, never change your routine.

567 ❖ Look busy.

568 ❖ Scalp tickets.

569 ❖ Outline his bald spot with your finger.

570 ❖ If you sprinkle when you tinkle, just leave it.

571 ❖ Pull the rug out from under someone.

572 ❖ Collect Sweet 'n Low from restaurants.

573 ❖ Tell your friend about her surprise party.

574 ❖ Have all the answers.

575 ❖ Suggest to mourners that they cheer up and look on the bright side.

576 ❖ Shuffle someone else's alphabetical file.

577 ❖ Tickle people.

578 ❖ Say you're sorry in a cheerful, lilting voice.

579 ❖ Slap people on the back.

580 ❖ Bite into the piece of fruit before offering it to someone else.

581 ❖ Show up late.

582 ❖ Leave early.

583 ❖ Ride your bike on crowded sidewalks.

584 ❖ Blow straw wrappers over to the folks at the next table.

585 ❖ Recommend that she shave her legs more often.

586 ❖ Crash your way into a parking space.

587 ❖ Be in contempt of court.

588 ❖ Bear false witness.

589 ❖ "Shoot" the messenger.

590 ❖ Leave your name in wet cement.

591 ❖ Break hearts, wind, and rules.

592 ❖ Bring pizza and beer to the Intensive Care Unit.

593 ❖ Tell your children that babies come from storks.

594 ❖ When you get close to celebrities, rip off a piece of their clothing.

595 ❖ Contradict your spouse loudly in public.

596 ❖ The phonier the better.

597 ❖ Ask very personal questions.

598 ❖ Take advantage of everyone.

599 ❖ Play mind games.

600 ❖ Don't replace the toilet paper roll.

601 ❖ Preach gloom and doom.

602 ❖ Throw your money around.

603 ❖ Quote Rush Limbaugh to feminists.

604 ❖ Give your friends' names to mailing lists and phone sales people.

605 ❖ Insist that people search for things that aren't lost.

606 ❖ Get one of those "Theme from The Godfather" car horns.

607 ❖ Practice misanthropy and misogyny.

608 ❖ Go ahead even when you know you are making a mistake.

609 ❖ Go to bed angry.

610 ❖ If you can't bedazzle then with your brilliance, baffle them with your bullshit.

611 ❖ Try getting away with murder.

612 ❖ If that doesn't work, try mayhem.

613 ❖ Suggest nose jobs to your friends.

614 ❖ Don't know and don't care.

615 ❖ Lash out at people who are only trying to help.

616 ❖ An ounce of cure is worth a pound of prevention.

617 ❖ Mail the postcards after you get back from vacation.

618 ❖ Delve into things that are none of your business.

619 ❖ Fill out deposit slips at the teller window.

620 ❖ See how tall and yellow your lawn grass can get.

621 ❖ Touch the tip of your shoes against the heels of the person on line in front of you.

622 ❖ Create warring factions in your family.

623 ❖ Ask them to name all 54 flavors, then order vanilla.

624 ❖ Believe you are above the law.

625 ❖ Lean back and look at your visitor through a thin, cold smile.

626 ❖ No need to say please or thank you.

627 ❖ Love is never having to say you're sorry.

628 ❖ Moan and groan.

629 ❖ Doubletalk.

630 ❖ Count your chickens before they are conceived.

631 ❖ Play monkey in the middle with your little niece.

632 ❖ Split the bill only when your meal costs more.

633 ❖ When you scratch his back, avoid the spot that itches.

634 ❖ Reserve the chaise, and then go swimming all day.

635 ❖ Play Super Mario Brothers for hours and hours.

636 ❖ Toss and turn when you're sleeping over.

637 ❖ Serve children blue cheese dressing.

638 ❖ You're right. The world does revolve around you.

639 ❖ Put a video camera in the employee washroom.

640 ❖ Make a visitor stand.

641 ❖ Elbow your way through a crowd.

642 ❖ Nickel and dime them.

643 ❖ Don't hesitate: Show the contempt you feel.

644 ❖ Humiliate someone when you need to establish control.

645 ❖ Stop and stare at accidents.

646 ❖ Tell everyone to prove it.

647 ❖ Prop your feet up on the boss's desk.

648 ❖ Borrow receipts to take to the IRS audit.

649 ❖ Slip a foul word by the vanity license plate censors.

650 ❖ Weave in and out of traffic just for fun.

651 ❖ Never let it be good enough.

652 ❖ Always play devil's advocate.

653 ❖ Wear a string bikini on the Stair Master.

654 ❖ Rapidly blurt out your address to someone who is writing it down.

655 ❖ Stop as soon as you get off the escalator.

656 ❖ Tell your co-worker you overheard a plan to fire him.

657 ❖ Leave a note from the tooth fairy, "Out of cash."

658 ❖ Tell him that you bought a false Rolex just like his.

659 ❖ Point out that her necklace plays up her double chin.

660 ❖ Allow every man his say, then contradict it.

661 ❖ Invite them for dinner and don't be home.

662 ❖ When you're really needed, leave town.

663 ❖ Eat garlic bread before your dentist appointment.

664 ❖ Leave the soap on the shower floor.

665 ❖ Pollute.

666 ❖ Lie in confession.

667 ❖ Tell tall tales.

668 ❖ Forget to spray the bathroom deodorizer.

669 ❖ Leave your messes for someone else to clean up.

670 ❖ Recommend an inept financial advisor.

671 ❖ Entertain flight passengers with crash stories.

672 ❖ Toss paper towels in the public toilet.

673 ❖ Adjust the reception while he's watching the big game.

674 ❖ Blow your nose at the dinner table.

675 ❖ Pull lint from his belly button.

676 ❖ Wipe off your eye make-up on the guest towels.

677 ❖ Tell a sick person about people you know who died.

678 ❖ Squeak chalk across the blackboard.

679 ❖ Tap their stemware to see if it rings.

680 ❖ When you meet people, make it clear you're sizing them up.

681 ❖ Don't come when you're called.

682 ❖ Keep on talking and talking and talking.

683 ❖ Have a cow.

684 ❖ Play dirty pool.

685 ❖ Always aim low.

686 ❖ Pick your nose and eat it.

687 ❖ When the doctor says, "Cough," spit.

688 ❖ Kiss and tell.

689 ❖ Act like a dweeb in front of your daughter's friends.

690 ❖ Ignore your call waiting.

691 ❖ "Borrow" other people's pens and pencils.

692 ❖ Mispronounce a colleague's name — for eleven years.

693 ❖ Leave a few stones unturned.

694 ❖ When your co-worker asks if you like his new haircut, cough.

695 ❖ Speed up after you pass the radar.

696 ❖ Pop a child's balloon.

697 ❖ Tell filthy jokes.

698 ❖ Hover aggressively over hors d'oeuvres.

699 ❖ Throw recyclables into the regular trash.

700 ❖ Go ahead: Ask what your country can do for you.

701 ❖ Always say never.

702 ❖ Eat ice cream in front of the children and don't share.

703 ❖ Plead poverty.

704 ❖ Leave a long message on your answering machine.

705 ❖ Fall asleep on jury duty.

706 ❖ Ask people how they got their limp.

707 ❖ Fire well before you see the whites of their eyes.

708 ❖ Groan when you sit down.

709 ❖ Groan when you stand up.

710 ❖ Do don't's and don't do do's.

711 ❖ Say "uh-oh" a lot.

712 ❖ Don't give an inch.

713 ❖ Try on underwear in stores.

714 ❖ Name your new baby Rothschild.

715 ❖ Return from the office john exclaiming: "Boy, that Feen-a-Mint really works."

716 ❖ Examine your Kleenex carefully after use.

717 ❖ Confuse first and second wives.

718 ❖ Leave skates on the stairs.

719 ❖ After the first person gives you directions, turn and ask someone else.

720 ❖ If an excuse is good enough to use once, it's good enough to use again.

721 ❖ Ask people to tell you again how their pet died.

722 ❖ In the locker room, stare at people as they undress.

723 ❖ Knock on limousine windows and peer inside.

724 ❖ Tell new neighbors that the neighborhood's gone downhill.

725 ❖ Dial a wrong number in the middle of the night — twice.

726 ❖ Squeeze your boyfriends' pimples.

727 ❖ A little white lie never hurt anyone.

LIFE'S LITTLE WHITE LIES AND EXCUSES

Knowing how to tell a little lie is integral to getting by in life....

728 ❖ Read my lips.

729 ❖ I'll ask my manager, but I doubt it.

730 ❖ Gee, I guess the invitation was just lost in the mail.

731 ❖ I thought you said you would take care of it.

732 ❖ I'm serious, you look great in that hat.

733 ❖ Have you lost weight?

734 ❖ No problem.

735 ❖ I'll call you.

736 ❖ Take my word for it.

737 ❖ Relax, nothing will go wrong.

738 ❖ Money back guarantee.

739 ❖ I never got the fax.

740 ❖ I'm not angry; I'm not mad.

741 ❖ I'm about to go into a meeting.

742 ❖ I ran into a lot of traffic.

743 ❖ You'll have to pay because I forgot my wallet.

744 ❖ I rarely drink this much.

745 ❖ David's parents said that he could.

746 ❖ I had to go to a funeral.

747 ❖ I'll keep your resume on file.

748 ❖ This wrinkle cream actually reverses aging.

749 ❖ You're too good for me.

750 ❖ This is my last piece of cake.

751 ❖ I'd do it for you.

752 ❖ I gave at the office.

753 ❖ One adult and four children, please.

754 ❖ Next time it's on me.

755 ❖ I promise not to tell anyone — ever.

756 ❖ My answering machine is broken, and I never got the message.

757 ❖ I was just going to call you.

758 ❖ You can trust me.

759 ❖ This hurts me more than it hurts you.

760 ❖ No offense.

761 ❖ Let me make this perfectly clear.

762 ❖ I am not a crook.

763 ❖ May the best person win.

764 ❖ I'm a size 6.

765 ❖ "All the taste of butter without the calories."

766 ❖ This is for your own good.

767 ❖ You'll see, this medicine tastes just like cherry syrup.

768 ❖ I never saw him before in my life.

769 ❖ "I never found Anita Hill attractive."

770 ❖ Honey, I have to work late.

771 ❖ He hit me first.

772 ❖ It was good for me, too.

773 ❖ It's not the money; I love working in the law.

774 ❖ I hear my mother calling me.

775 ❖ Actually, I like the taste of tofu.

776 ❖ It feels so good to be single again.

777 ❖ It's one-of-a-kind.

778 ❖ It's nothing personal, I'm just not interested in dating right now.

779 ❖ It's so simple a child can do it.

780 ❖ I'm really glad you got that off your chest.

781 ❖ I'm just on my way out the door.

782 ❖ My grandmother died. (Again.)

783 ❖ I must be losing my memory.

784 ❖ It's in mint condition.

785 ❖ I knew that.

786 ❖ I never eat. Why am I so fat?

787 ❖ Oh, I thought it was tomorrow night.

788 ❖ This time, I mean it.

789 ❖ You're my favorite
mother-in-law.

790 ❖ I never said that.

791 ❖ I won't make the same mistake again.

792 ❖ I was never told.

793 ❖ You're my best friend in the whole wide world.

794 ❖ I love you.

795 ❖ I love you, too.

796 ❖ If I had to lose, I'm glad you won.

797 ❖ The dog ate my homework.

798 ❖ Please don't take this the wrong way, but....

799 ❖ Sorry, my car broke down.

800 ❖ I didn't feel a thing.

801 ❖ Studies show....

802 ❖ Easy to assemble.

803 ❖ I was only teasing.

804 ❖ I'll be right with you.

805 ❖ We're just good friends.

806 ❖ I followed directions.

807 ❖ I'm not lying. Honest.

808 ❖ That's the cutest baby I've ever seen.

809 ❖ I can't believe that's a toupee — it looks so natural.

810 ❖ I have no idea how this got broken.

811 ❖ I'd love to see more baby pictures.

812 ❖ I'll just go back to sleep for five more minutes.

813 ❖ I'm just smoking to keep my weight down.

814 ❖ I love to have the grandchildren visit.

815 ❖ Honey, that was the best meatloaf I've ever had.

816 ❖ I really only watch PBS.

817 ❖ Back in the old days, I was a handsome devil.

818 ❖ I don't mind sleeping on the floor.

819 ❖ No, I don't mind staying until 9 P.M.

820 ❖ Diet shakes are so satisfying.

821 ❖ I didn't want it, anyway.

822 ❖ I'd love to stay and help, but I have to be somewhere.

823 ❖ Keep driving; I think I know where we are now.

824 ❖ I'd like to still be friends.

825 ❖ It's an honor to meet you, Mr. Quayle.

826 ❖ What grey hair?

827 ❖ There's a swimsuit to flatter every figure.

828 ❖ My home is your home — stay as long as you like.

829 ❖ I've chosen a bridesmaid dress that you all can wear again.

830 ❖ "Handsome, athletic, intelligent, sensitive, SWM seeks...."

831 ❖ Tastes just like homemade.

832 ❖ ☺Have a nice day.

LIFE'S LITTLE SELF DESTRUCTIONS

When you're through ragging on everyone else, there's only one person left to torture....

833 ❖ Apologize even if you didn't do anything.

834 ❖ Apologize for living.

835 ❖ Apologize for apologizing.

836 ❖ Live in a constant state of denial.

837 ❖ Don't buckle your seat belt — you're only going for a quick drive.

838 ❖ Forget to sign your Christmas cards.

839 ❖ Lock your keys in the car.

840 ❖ Monopolize the most boring person at a dinner party.

841 ❖ Step off the curb without checking for puddles.

842 ❖ Drive to the Poconos for your free gift.

843 ❖ As you introduce your husband, forget his name.

844 ❖ Shoot a whole roll without any film.

845 ❖ Break a mirror.

846 ❖ Stand on rickety old chairs.

847 ❖ Need to be in two places at once.

848 ❖ Tell your friends to drop by your summer home any weekend.

849 ❖ Leap before you look.

850 ❖ Change your mind.

851 ❖ Change it back.

852 ❖ Delay until it's too late.

853 ❖ Write a nasty letter to the I.R.S.

854 ❖ Bawl out a cop while he's writing you a ticket.

855 ❖ Suggest meeting your blind date at a topless bar.

856 ❖ Describe your sex life to your in-laws.

857 ❖ If something goes wrong, eat a whole bag of potato chips.

858 ❖ If you go up to the limit on your credit card, get another one.

859 ❖ Bite your nails while you are waiting.

860 ❖ If at first you don't succeed, cry.

861 ❖ If you don't come from a dysfunctional family, make one up.

862 ❖ Unload your problems on your kids.

863 ❖ Compare yourself to others for that greater than/less than feeling.

864 ❖ List your membership in AA on your resume.

865 ❖ Start that long drive home when you're drowsy.

866 ❖ When the relationship is definitely over, try to make it work again.

867 ❖ When he cheats on you, make it up to him.

868 ❖ See an ineffectual psychiatrist for years.

869 ❖ Support your friend's coke habit.

870 ❖ Hide the bottle in plain sight.

871 ❖ Let every stranger control your life.

872 ❖ Say yes when you mean no.

873 ❖ Buy yet another diet book.

874 ❖ If you're not the oppressor, be the victim.

875 ❖ Work for your ex.

876 ❖ Spend all your holidays with your parents.

877 ❖ Be a wallflower.

878 ❖ Walk with your eyes down.

879 ❖ Nap during your therapy session.

880 ❖ Always let people go ahead of you on line.

881 ❖ Wake up and smell the manure.

882 ❖ Rationalize away your problems.

883 ❖ Make up your mind and don't change.

884 ❖ Never look people in the eye.

885 ❖ Wear white when you have your period.

886 ❖ Buy a vowel that's been called already.

887 ❖ Spend more than you earn.

888 ❖ Agree with everyone else all the time.

889 ❖ Make important life decisions by flipping a coin.

890 ❖ Tell different lies to different people until you forget what the truth is.

891 ❖ Tell people you're recovering.

892 ❖ Only see one solution.

893 ❖ Ask people who don't like you for help.

894 ❖ Don't feel your feelings.

895 ❖ Heave a sigh and do what they want anyway.

896 ❖ Be assertive ... NOT!

897 ❖ Always mount a horse on its right side.

898 ❖ Pull on an itchy tag and rip the collar.

899 ❖ Set your alarm clock for 6:00 P.M. the night before your big job interview.

900 ❖ Buy expensive things on impulse.

901 ❖ Sit directly down on the public toilet seat without looking first.

902 ❖ If you're ever lucky enough to meet the Queen of England, give her a big hug.

903 ❖ Order pesto fettucini with lobster at a job interview lunch.

904 ❖ Forget your passport.

905 ❖ After the second date, move in together.

906 ❖ Wear pastel blue leisure suits and white loafers.

907 ❖ Pack heavy groceries into flimsy bags.

908 ❖ Enter a beauty pageant.

909 ❖ Let life pass you by.

910 ❖ Ignore expiration dates on prescription bottles.

911 ❖ Blame yourself for everyone else's problems.

912 ❖ Flip off your computer before saving your work.

913 ❖ Load up on goodies for "unexpected company."

914 ❖ Tape a stupid TV show over your all-time favorite movie.

915 ❖ Machine wash your silk dress.

916 ❖ Invite your mother-in-law for a visit when your mother is already ensconced in the guest room.

917 ❖ Sit next to the fattest person on a long distance bus trip.

918 ❖ Believe him when he says his wife doesn't understand him.

919 ❖ Flush your diamond engagement ring down the toilet to prove you're angry with him.

920 ❖ Save that snapshot that makes you look like a cow.

921 ❖ Call him every ten minutes.

922 ❖ Send an expensive wedding gift but forget to include your name.

923 ❖ Leave your sex toys around when the cleaning lady comes.

924 ❖ Bring your talkative friend along to a silent retreat.

925 ❖ Try a complicated new recipe for your last minute dinner party.

926 ❖ Call in sick and then go lunch-time shopping right near your office.

927 ❖ Just for a change, walk home down the dark, narrow alley.

928 ❖ Jump in the shower with no towel in sight.

929 ❖ Order a diet cola with a huge scoop of ice cream.

930 ❖ So you're allergic, eat it anyway.

931 ❖ Loan your friend money just one more time.

932 ❖ Arrive at the airport five minutes before your international flight.

933 ❖ Ask a chronic complainer, "How are you?"

934 ❖ Rent the apartment over a night club.

935 ❖ Decide to attend a college you've never visited.

936 ❖ Flaunt your infidelity.

937 ❖ Forget to check the gas tank.

938 ❖ Forget to lock the bathroom booth.

939 ❖ Add chlorine bleach to the colored wash.

940 ❖ Attempt to break up a fight on the subway.

941 ❖ Buy running shoes without trying them on.

942 ❖ Sit home on a Saturday night and wait for his call.

943 ❖ Clean your loaded handgun.

944 ❖ In front of the children.

945 ❖ Assume the bank NEVER makes a mistake.

946 ❖ Keep your money under your mattress.

947 ❖ Be the designated driver when drinks are on the house.

948 ❖ Enjoy a huge meal before you ride the roller coaster.

949 ❖ Call 900 numbers and talk for hours.

950 ❖ Threaten your kids with, "Wait until Daddy gets home."

951 ❖ Let your makeup cake — especially blue eyeshadow.

952 ❖ Belabor a point.

953 ❖ Belabor a point.

954 ❖ Talk toofast.

955 ❖ Don't pay your bookie.

956 ❖ Kiss a frog and hope it becomes a prince.

957 ❖ Talk only about yourself on a first date.

958 ❖ Drink the water in Mexico.

959 ❖ Drink the contents of your finger bowl at a formal state dinner.

960 ❖ Get dressed in the dark.

961 ❖ Just say "Yes."

962 ❖ Ask to see more wedding pictures.

963 ❖ Eat more fried foods.

964 ❖ Pick your teeth with the business card a client has just handed you.

965 ❖ Pay extra for the one-hour drycleaning service and come back three weeks later to pick it up.

966 ❖ Have your lawyer contact the jurors to improve the odds of winning your suit.

967 ❖ Appear on a Hair Club for Men commercial.

968 ❖ Don't name your computer files.

969 ❖ Choose your career on the advice of a psychic.

970 ❖ Correct your boss in front of his peers.

971 ❖ Let the toddlers have as much chocolate as they want.

972 ❖ Mail important letters by fourth class mail.

973 ❖ Volunteer your apartment for the wedding.

974 ❖ Obsess over a celebrity.

975 ❖ Drink coffee close to bedtime.

976 ❖ Tear up a photo of the Pope on national television.

977 ❖ Binge and purge.

978 ❖ Look for true love in the personal ads.

979 ❖ Tuck your skirt into your pantyhose after using the bathroom.

980 ❖ Make a pass at your sister's husband.

981 ❖ Joke about shooting the president while in line for the White House tour.

982 ❖ Rely on your memory.

983 ❖ Load up on prunes before a hot date.

984 ❖ Stick the bubbling hot pizza right in your mouth.

985 ❖ Plead ignorance.

986 ❖ Walk under a ladder.

987 ❖ Stop using four letter words and try labels like cretin, doofus, and nerd.

988 ❖ Get a job making cold calls at the dinner hour.

989 ❖ Overreact.

990 ❖ Wear underwear that creeps up.

991 ❖ Be codependent.

992 ❖ Make promises you can't possibly keep.

993 ❖ Miss two car payments.

994 ❖ Toilet train her before she's ready.

995 ❖ Pick up the check all the time.

996 ❖ Play with fire.

997 ❖ When he asks for all the details, tell him.

998 ❖ Ask for trouble.

999 ❖ Play hard to get
when you want to
get got.

1000 ❖ Bake like a flounder in the hot summer sun.

1001 ❖ Hang your pocketbook over the back of your chair in crowded restaurants.

1002 ❖ Put the wrong letters in the wrong envelopes.

1003 ❖ Play with your vegetables.

1004 ❖ Cut in front of New York City taxi cabs.

1005 ❖ Whenever your child whines for a new toy, buy it.

1006 ❖ Leave the tube of black shoe polish near the toothpaste.

1007 ❖ Look on the dark side.

1008 ❖ Cross your fingers when you tell a lie.

1009 ❖ Ward off evil spirits with garlic.

1010 ❖ Let people wipe their feet on you.

1011 ❖ Have the foggiest idea.

1012 ❖ Step out on the ledge to wash the high-rise windows.

1013 ❖ Don't do today what you can put off until tomorrow.

1014 ❖ Press your luck.

1015 ❖ Skate on thin ice.

1016 ❖ Judge a book by its cover.

1017 ❖ Don't replace the spare.

1018 ❖ Open mouth. Insert foot.

1019 ❖ Wear diamonds, gold necklaces, and furs on the subway.

1020 ❖ Try to please all of the people all of the time.

1021 ❖ Seek out negative influences.

1022 ❖ Believe everything you read.

1023 ❖ Mull it over in the middle of the night.

1024 ❖ Spend the day at the Motor Vehicle Bureau.

1029 ❖ Insist on having the last word.

1025 ❖ Break up; go back; break up; go back.

1026 ❖ Go to work with a little tissue on your chin.

1027 ❖ Keep imagining everything else that can go wrong.

1028 ❖ Ask for a haircut when you want a trim.